LOOKING for CRABS

*To Rosie for her inspiration
and constant support*

An Angus & Robertson Publication

Angus&Robertson, an imprint of
HarperCollins*Publishers*
25 Ryde Road, Pymble, Sydney, NSW 2073, Australia
31 View Road, Glenfield, Auckland 10, New Zealand
10 East 53rd Street, New York NY 10022, USA

First published in Australia in 1992
Book Club edition 1992
This Bluegum paperback edition published in 1993
Reprinted 1993 (twice), 1994

National Library of Australia
Cataloguing-in-Publication data:

Whatley, Bruce.
  Looking for crabs.
  ISBN 0 207 17771 6 (p/b)
  1. Crabs – Juvenile literature. I. Title.
595.3842.

Printed in Hong Kong
10 9 8 7 6 5
97 96 95 94

LOOKING for CRABS

BRUCE WHATLEY

Angus&Robertson
An imprint of HarperCollinsPublishers

I love going to the beach for holidays.
Sometimes it's too cold to swim
so we go looking for crabs.

Rock pools are a great place
to look for crabs,
but you have to be very quiet.

Crabs can be difficult to find.
You have to look really hard,
but try not to scare them!

Dad says crabs are usually found
under little rocks
at the bottom of rock pools.

Mum says you have to tread carefully
so you don't hurt them.

But I don't think there can be
any crabs at our beach.

Even when Dad lifted up
a really big rock
we didn't find any.

Mum said they were probably out to lunch,
but I think they were just hiding.

Crabs are very good at hiding.
I couldn't see any in my little pool.

Sometimes you find hermit crabs
living in little shells.
But not when we were on holiday.

Where do they go in the holidays?
Dad suggested Hawaii.

My little sister said Disneyland.
I told them we just weren't
looking hard enough.

I don't know where the crabs go
in the holidays.
But one thing I do know . . .

There are no crabs at our beach!